Ju
F
Is 3   Ish-Kishor, Sulamith.
          Drusilla.

DRUSILLA

DRUSILLA

A NOVEL OF THE EMPEROR HADRIAN

BY SULAMITH ISH-KISHOR

DRAWINGS BY THOMAS MORLEY

PANTHEON BOOKS

Translation from Pervigilium Veneris by Sulamith Ish-Kishor.

FOR BRUNO
Livia and Luciano

ACKNOWLEDGEMENTS

To the American Numismatic Society
To P. Califano

To the New York Public Library, Research Libraries
Fifth Avenue and 42nd Street, New York City —

and

To the kind of editor that writers dream about

NOTE

An Emperor or his chosen heir automatically was given the name Caesar in memory of Julius Caesar, who lived about 150 years before Hadrian. An Emperor was usually addressed by this title, Caesar, or Domine Caesar, my lord Caesar.

All Romans of any importance had three names. Hadrian's full name was Publius (first name) Aelius (family name) Hadrianus (which really meant "lord of Hadria," or Adria, the strip of land on the Adriatic coast of Italy where his ancestors had lived).

A Roman Emperor was not necessarily succeeded by his next of kin. He could choose his heir by a form of legal adoption. His adoptive "son" could be of any age at all.

The Romans counted the years from the founding of the city of Rome, *"ab urbe condita,"* using the initials A.U.C. Rome was founded in 753 B.C. So our year A.D. 1 is the year of Rome 754. Hadrian reigned from A.D. 117 to A.D. 138, or from 870 A.U.C. to 891 A.U.C.

The ninth hour, in summertime, was from about half-past two in the afternoon till about a quarter to four. The Romans were never very accurate about the time of day.

After Hadrian's death, when Marcus Annius Verus Aurelius became, together with Titus Antoninus, one of the next Caesars, the Senate voted to popularize his name as Marcus Aurelius.

DRUSILLA

But I don't *believe* what Marius is saying!

I *can't* believe it!

He comes up to me with "You're such a naïve little thing, Drusilla," and "But I told you so, Drusilla," and bowls me over with a piece of news like that—and then does he really expect me to take it like a lamb—when I am morally certain it can't be true?

After all, I'm not in love with Marius, and he has no right to lecture me on what I ought to feel about other people, even if he is older than I am, and a boy.

He's never said a pleasant word about poor Fuscus—always about his faults. Who hasn't got faults? When I first saw Fuscus I was only a child—that was in the year of Rome 883—and Fuscus was in his teens, and everybody knows a boy his age wouldn't pay any attention to a child, but Fuscus was just like a friend to me.

Even then, I couldn't help feeling sorry for Fuscus; he was thin, with his head always leaning to one side, and his mother was dead, and he missed her. I know he's supposed to be very arrogant and fussy about his rank, but I saw him alone in the imperial gardens once and he was crying. Even though he's the Emperor's grandnephew and heir to the empire—if you want to think of the republic that way; some do and some don't—but still he's young and he doesn't have anyone close, and I'm a half-orphan and I can imagine how terrible it must feel to be a whole orphan like Fuscus.

And now Marius calmly walks over from his garden to ours, and looks down at me, shielding his blue eyes from the morning sun—and I can see very clearly from their hard expression that he really isn't sorry at all—and says,

4

"I wish I didn't have to tell you this, Drusilla, but somebody will have to. Servianus is condemned to death for plotting against the life of the Emperor. . . ."

He knows I despise that old villain Servianus as much as anyone else does, so there must be something else. I couldn't help holding my breath—

"And—what about Fuscus?"

"Fuscus too."

"*Oh*! But why? Why Fuscus? Just because he's the grandson of the old brute? Could he help that?"

"Drusilla," said Marius, "do you really think our Emperor would condemn a young man to die if he didn't have good reason?"

"Reason! How can there be reason for anything so cruel? Fuscus was always under the thumb of Servianus—he just did what Servianus made him do, *he* never really did anything. You always think everything Emperor Hadrian does is right—"

"I thought *you* were the one who adores Hadrian like a god."

"Well, I do. He's great, he's just—but he *could* make a mistake, couldn't he, especially if a person he condemns hasn't a true friend in the world to speak up for him—and Fuscus never had, because nobody likes Servianus."

Marius looked simply overcome.

"Honestly, Drusilla—! You never think. You only feel. Anyone can tell from that flat little nose of yours! You're Greek and Greek women don't think!"

"What has my nose to do with it!"

"My teacher Fronto at the Academy thinks Hadrian is absolutely right. Great Jupiter! Servianus is ninety-two years old, he's been a senator for ages, and all the time that he's known Hadrian he's been plotting against him!"

"Of course. Nobody doubts that. But how could Fuscus, who's only nineteen—"

"Fuscus has been right along with him, all the time, that's what you don't see."

"But he hasn't!"

I *knew* it, for suddenly there flashed on my mind a recollection!

A scene on a ship . . . voices clearly heard in a fog . . . an old voice relentlessly driving, scolding, insisting . . . a young voice whining, pleading, opposing . . .

Of course!

Hadrian didn't know about that!

I can prove it. I myself overheard it. I am the only one who has this proof. And I can tell the Emperor.

I must go to Caesar.

I shall save the life of a young man, an innocent young man, and my friend. More than that, I shall save our great Emperor from committing an injustice that would forever darken his name in history.

I have to wait for my father to come home. I need him to arrange it for me. He's a senator and

6

also he's head of a Sacred College of Augurs who foretell which days are going to be lucky and which are not, and besides, he's been a friend of Caesar's for many years.

It seems strange that Hadrian's own sister's grandson should be mixed up in anything like this, but everyone knows what can happen in families, especially when they're very rich and important. I suppose his sister wasn't much to brag about, or she wouldn't have married Servianus, who was ages older than she, when she knew he was Hadrian's worst enemy.

Yes, she did know, because everybody knew. Servianus was always doing nasty things to Hadrian. One time though it rebounded against Servianus! That's long before I was born, but the story got around and it's still being laughed over. It happened that the old Emperor Nerva, who had adopted Trajan as his heir, died rather suddenly. Trajan was then with the army in the north, and Hadrian was commanding the troops in the east. Hadrian naturally wanted to be the first to congratulate Trajan on becoming Emperor.

Servianus didn't want Hadrian to get there before him or, rather, before his messengers, because he was even then too old to rush anywhere himself. So he bribed some of the soldiers to saw through half the axle of Hadrian's war-chariot, so that it would break down on the way and leave him stranded.

Well, the army would never let Servianus get the best of Hadrian. But these troopers wanted the gold pieces Servianus offered them. So the man took the money and they went and sawed only partly through the axle, so that when it broke it would be not very far from the camp of Trajan. And when Hadrian's chariot couldn't go further and his companions told him it was the axle and it couldn't be mended in time, Hadrian just jumped down and marched the rest of the way.

And he got there first, and brought Trajan the news that he was the new emperor, and congratulated him, and Trajan was so pleased that he gave Hadrian the big diamond ring which old Nerva had given to him, as a token that he would pick Hadrian as his own heir.

And how did it happen that Hadrian got there first, walking, when Servianus' messengers were riding? Simply that the messengers picked the very longest route around! And they didn't hurry themselves! There was absolutely nothing Servianus could do about it.

The reason the army idolizes Hadrian isn't only that he's a great general, and that he used to march with his troops and eat with them and live as they did—he never ordered them to take any risk that he didn't take himself, like when he swam across the Danube River with the troopers when he, being the general, could have walked over a narrow little bridge that was there; he had to be helped to climb ashore by younger men.

The main thing is that he is always just and fair to everyone, no matter whom he likes or whom he dislikes. And that's the most important thing to soldiers. They always knew they could trust him.

And that's one reason I'm certain that if I can only get Caesar to listen to me, I can save poor Fuscus.

When father walked in onto our terrace I saw at once that he was deeply troubled.

I hurried down to meet him. I took away his hooked priest's baton because that always makes me see him as the mysterious prophecy-making augur rather than as the dear man he is. I kissed his hand; he tried to smile, and he kissed my forehead. ·

He sat down, rather heavily, at the little marble table. I clapped for a slave to bring us all a refreshing cool drink.

He nodded to Marius, then sighed deeply.

"Greetings, Senator and Augur," Marius said. "I suppose you've just come from the Senate. You know the news."

"Go inside, my little honey-cup," father told me. "Those little red-gold curls are all tousled."

"I know already what has happened," I exclaimed.

"You shouldn't have told her, Marius. . . . I'm

afraid we may be on the verge of—a very bad period. The Senate is furious."

"Why, I thought they hated the old brute! Who likes Servianus?" Marius demanded.

"Nobody . . . but he is a senator. If the Emperor can condemn a senator to summary execution—"

"Summary!" The word hit me like a blow.

"But there's no time for trials," Marius exclaimed. "There may be another attempt on Caesar's life at any time—"

"The argument may be correct. But they are afraid. Many say that Hadrian is going back to his old bad ways—as at the time of his accession, when the four ex-consuls were caught and executed—"

"But, Senator! They had plotted to murder him! And everybody thought Servianus was behind it. The ex-consuls weren't killed at *Caesar's* orders. It's known that Hadrian wanted them tried; it was his old Praefect of the Praetorian Guard who did it—"

"Well, they said so—"

"Yes, the Praefect got scared and had them killed—"

"But," said father, "Caesar swore at the time that he would never put a senator to death."

"He never has, till now," said Marius. "That's almost twenty years. Servianus still wants to be Emperor. And it's still possible, if Hadrian should die before Servianus."

"The Senate will never forgive the execution of a senator."

It suddenly struck me then that father might be more willing than I had hoped, to help me get to Caesar.

And I was right.

I had to wait one more terrible hour, while a slave hurried to the Imperial Palace and came back with the wax tablet signed by Diotimos, Caesar's personal valet, that the lady Drusilla Vera Aureliana, daughter of Drusus Verus, senator and head of a sacred college of Augurs, would be admitted tomorrow at the ninth hour to the presence of Hadrian Caesar.

At the bottom of the tablet I noticed another few words: "Cut it short."

Good. I shall have an excuse for my father that I was able to speak only for Fuscus, not for Servianus.

I am sitting now, in the radiant sunshine of a beautiful afternoon, on a plaza in the gardens overlooking the widespread city, its marble temples, its flowered parks, the winding brown Tiber, the huge new Mausoleum, sparkly white, with the purple-spotted marble pillars around that throw like a veil of violet, its statues and white marble bridge, and the ancient mass of tenements beyond.

In two hours I am to speak with the Emperor.

My heart is beating like a flying bird held back.

I feel so eager to rush to Caesar with all I can tell him. If Fuscus only knew now that he was not to die, after all . . . I would like to spare him that agony. Poor boy, I know how little happiness his life has held for him.

Two of our menservants are attending me. I would not let Marius come; I know he'd only keep trying to weaken me. Yes, I know he's devoted to me—he says he has never even thought about other girls, ever since we met at the Greek city of Oxyrhynchos, on Hadrian's Nile journey . . .

That was more than five years ago.

And that's where I first met Fuscus, too.

I think now what really drew me to Fuscus at the start was when they told me he hadn't either father or mother. I had been through a terrible time, when I was about five.

Papa is a Roman and he was on a visit to Athens and he met mama and he teased her about her red hair (Greeks think red hair unlucky but it was red-gold actually) and he said you could see her a mile away like a house on fire and she cried and he begged her pardon and they were married. And it was so long before I came that he told her all right, he would be satisfied even with a red-haired girl instead of a dark Roman son, and then a year later I was born, and they used to laugh over that so much!

They were very happy and it seems to me I was never out of the arms of one or the other, and Marius says that is what ruined me. And then mama suddenly went out of the world, and papa was utterly different for a long time; I was not allowed even to go near him, he was in a separate room all the time and physicians came and the whole household was in a state. I'll never forget the terror and the bitter black loneliness of that time.

Then Caesar sent him his own physician, the Greek Hermogenes; most people said Hermogenes had crazy ideas but Caesar said they were not crazy ideas, they were new ideas, and anyhow papa got better and one day I came into his room and he was sitting up and when he saw me all the light came back into his eyes and he said, "My life has come back to me."

So when they told me Fuscus hadn't anyone, my heart went right out to him.

I am rather nervous about speaking to Caesar, because he is a man who is always very sure of what he is doing. But I believe too that he isn't the kind of person who can't be told a new fact even if it doesn't fit in with what he has already decided.

14

And besides, every time I've been among the people of his court—in a way I mean that he would notice me—he has always been very kind. He is very patient with children and women, with everybody really, only he does lose his temper if stupid people try to take advantage.

They've told me that when I was first shown to him—he likes to have the new children brought to see him—I was about two, and I gripped hold of his thumb and wouldn't let go, and he laughed and made a joke. But when father and Aunt Bibi showed me to the Empress Sabina I didn't want to kiss her and I don't think she ever liked me after that. She was always pale and cold-looking, with her hair done so pompously I always wondered how she could make a movement without bringing it down! You felt you could never get past all those stiff curls and jewels.

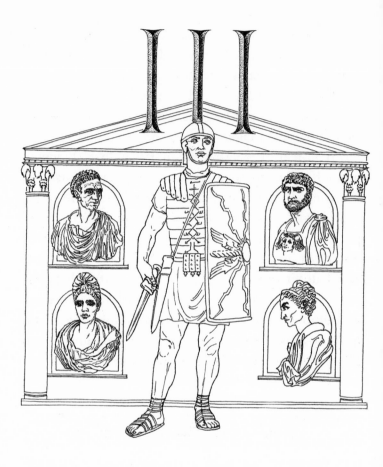

Hadrian knows what it feels like to be falsely accused, and held responsible for terrible things when you have not done them.

Even now, though he was supposedly entirely cleared of any blame in the killing of the four ex-consuls, those who had any doubts at all of him will begin dragging up that old story.

I wonder too why he didn't go after Servianus at that time; the old bear was known to be doing everything he could and spending fortunes to get adopted by Trajan, but he was too ridiculously old for it even then, in 870. As for Trajan's wife, Plotina, she thought him a snake.

But some people say Hadrian couldn't touch Servianus because the old man knew a secret—about Hadrian—that might have come out in the wash.

And it is true that Trajan never really cared for Hadrian. They were cousins, though Trajan was lots older, and people said Trajan envied him because he was so handsome and had a brilliant mind and a marvelous memory and made everybody like him, and he was just as good a soldier as Trajan, too.

Also maybe because Trajan's young wife, Plotina —she was a real lady and everyone respected her— she had brought up Hadrian. This may seem strange, but his mother sent him to her in Rome when he was only ten. The Aelii family are Spanish-born, descendants of Roman veterans settled there near the river Baetis by General Scipio Africanus three hundred years ago (everyone knows the Aelii were accepted because of their wealth, but Hadrian isn't *quite* a patrician, like the Veri or the Aureliani, who descend from the Founding Fathers of Rome).

Well it seems Hadrian's mother was very beautiful but poor and she knew the elder Hadrian only married her to have a son and heir to carry on his name, so she hated her husband and didn't care

17

about her son but only loved her daughter, and they were both nasty to him. And as soon as her husband died she sent the boy away. It's simply unbelievable what some people will do.

It turned out lucky for Hadrian, though, because Plotina had no children and she welcomed him with open arms. She seemed very majestic and serious but she was very kind and tender and wise. She thought young Hadrian the most wonderful boy in the world and she probably bored poor Trajan to death with how marvelous he was, and Hadrian worshiped the ground she walked on.

So no wonder if Trajan felt squeezed out between those two!

I don't suppose anybody felt like telling the Empress about the troubles her little angel got himself into, or when he grew up about his wild parties and his flirtations; Servianus did get hold of some unpaid bills of young Hadrian's and showed them to Trajan —the sneak!—but Trajan thought this was playing dirty and besides he had been just as bad when he was a youngster and Plotina knew it, so he just paid the bills himself—and was that "one in the eye" for Servianus!

Maybe Hadrian found out that Trajan knew a few things about him, because he became very serious in his work and then was given important city positions, and even was clerk of the Senate for a while, and he learned stenography for that and was very good at it. Then he served in the army as an ordinary soldier, marching with the troops and eating the same rations, doing the same work and the military exercises and all. So the soldiers all got to know him and he knew them and he never forgot anyone he met. When he became an officer they began to hope he would be the next Emperor.

Nobody could say that it was Empress Plotina who got promotions for him, because they knew he had worked his way up, though of course for him it went much faster than if he hadn't been the Emperor's cousin.

Trajan wanted him to get married, and it was Plotina who urged him to marry Trajan's niece, Vibia Sabina, and he did it though he wasn't in love with her at all. Sabina was rather pretty they said when she was a young girl, and she always dressed very finely, but she never liked anybody very much. I heard people say that Hadrian was more of a husband to Plotina than he ever was to Sabina, but I never knew what they meant by that. They were people who disliked Hadrian.

Then Trajan died in the army camp at Salinus and those people insisted he had never named anybody as his heir; his tent had been closed off the last three days of his life, and then Plotina had come out and showed them Trajan's will naming Hadrian as the next Emperor, as Caesar, and Commander in Chief of the armed forces.

Most of the people were pleased and the army went wild with joy. Some senators did want to start a row that Plotina had forged the will, and Servianus thought he might be able to come in on that, but after all, it isn't wise to argue with seventy thousand Legionaries, so they decided to keep their thoughts to themselves.

So Hadrian became Emperor.

But it hadn't been easy. And he knows what envious people can do, he knows what lies can be told, and what harm can be done to innocent people.

I can't understand why I should be trembling like this at the thought of speaking with Emperor Hadrian. He wants to be kind to everybody; he always says that he is merely "the first among his peers," because there must be somebody to be the final authority. He is only angry when stupid people don't know where to stop, and when they seem unable to understand that after all he must receive respect and deference.

And he was always specially kind to me when I was a child.

How it was that, being a young child, I was often in the presence of the Emperor, is simply this: my father and his family were in Athens, visiting the family of my mother after she passed away and he got over his illness.

The Emperor had recently set out on one of his long journeys; he felt it was his duty to visit and revisit the provinces, correcting bad conditions, rebuilding and restoring wherever it was needed, strengthening the frontiers—he wanted above all to keep peace and build up the cities. And he loved traveling, anyway; there was no place he wouldn't go if it was worthwhile; he even climbed Mount Casius, they said, to watch the sunrise from there, but he and his party got caught in a snowstorm. He never seemed to mind risking his life.

So now he was going on a long visit to the east, and he was going to sail up the Nile to try and discover its sources, hundreds of miles into Upper Egypt.

His ships put in at Athens, naturally; it's the city he loves best, because of its great art and all the philosophers and poets; you may jeer at him for a Greek-ist but you may be sure that if he had lived in their time he would never have let anyone touch a hair of the head of Socrates or Archimedes or Aristides—and he'd have roared with laughter over Diogenes searching with a lamp to find an honest man.

Well, the Athenians went crazy with joy when he came because we all knew he'd do us all kinds of benefit. That's when the new gate was started, with the lion on top, dividing the ancient part of the city from the magnificent new part he was planning— and the new city's getting *built*, too!

Father didn't take much part in the festivities as he was still not quite well, but he went to pay his respects of course to the Emperor, and he took me with him. I was still very sad about my mama, and when I was presented to Caesar I suppose he noticed it, he didn't just pat my head and say, "pretty little thing"; he knew something about medicine himself and he asked Hermogenes the physician if he didn't think I needed care, and Hermogenes thought I needed a complete change. So Hadrian suggested that my father join the imperial journey and bring me along.

Father couldn't go, I don't know why, but Empress Sabina was planning to set out soon, on her own ship, catching up with the Emperor's fleet at Alexandria in Egypt, where he was to stay for some weeks. Hadrian said I might have my two aunts—my father's sister Aunt Bibiena and my mother's sister

Aunt Chloe—come with me in care of Sabina and her court.

My aunts were overjoyed and my father had to give in and let me go. I didn't want to leave father but the Emperor said I must learn not to be afraid, and he took me on his knee and his face looked very kind and as if he knew how I felt; he is a very tall, well-built man with rough curly fair hair and a very short curly beard; they say he wears it out of vanity to hide a birthmark, well why shouldn't he? His eyes are gray and they can look hard and keen but that time they looked like my father's eyes, and I kissed his hand, and he smiled and kissed me on the forehead just the way papa does.

So I went on the ship when the Empress came.

The Emperor's fleet sailed off from Piraeus and they were a splendid sight, his own ship going first with purple sails and a lot of gold flashing all around it.

Next week the ship of the Empress Sabina came into port; she did not visit in Athens, and I said goodbye for a little while to my father, and my aunts and I went onto her ship and they brought me to the Empress.

The Lady Sabina was a very tall, dignified lady, awfully serious, and I was still afraid of her, even after my aunts presented me. Sabina nodded to me, then she smiled a little and asked what father's

24

augury for this voyage had been; it hadn't been very good, so my aunts said they didn't know, he hadn't made any. (And here Aunt Bibi was always telling me it was wrong to tell a lie! That's the way grown-ups treat children!) Then they said they thought it was a good augury!

The Empress touched some jewels she wore round her neck and she patted her side-curls—she had quite a pretty coiffure that day, I remember, a Greek woman had done it—but she looked rather grim anyway. She hoped I would improve in health —but the Nile! only a man would suggest that for a child's health, she said. Sabina had no children.

I'm trying to remember Alexandria now—somehow I can't; I simply realize that I'm sitting on this plaza in Rome, waiting for the ninth hour . . .

That old city of Alexandria . . . it was the noisiest place I've ever been in. The Twin Harbor was always full of ships putting in or going out, and all the crowds running about dressed in every kind of clothes from heavy wrapped-up national costumes to practically naked, so you thought some of them must be roasting in that hot sun and others freezing in the cool breeze that almost always blew.

And that terrific, high lighthouse, the Pharos—we went up it in a donkey-cart that took us round the ramps.

And it isn't true that they grow lots of flowers—the city is built on a granite island and all those late roses are imported!

I never could go out walking because there were little riots going on all the time: the Greek quarter fighting the Jewish quarter and daring them to set foot across the line; the Jews fighting both the Greeks and the low-class native Egyptians; the Egyptians in the ancient native quarter fighting the Romans and the Greeks and the Jews, and saying why didn't everybody get out of their country, and demanding self-government and at the same time saying Rome must go; and the Egyptian workers on strike because there weren't enough onions to go round—that's about all I can remember.

Except of course that we were taken to see the old palace of Julius Caesar and the ruins of the old Library that had been burned down by some fool and Hadrian was having it rebuilt, and we saw the golden sword of Alexander the Great and his tomb where he was still to be seen in a crystal sarcophagus —a body nearly five hundred years old, ugh, but the Egyptians loved having old bodies around.

Anyhow they were all very happy to have the Emperor come because it was good for business and also because he was frightening the Praefect of Egypt, whom they naturally hated, and making him reform the tax system and other matters.

Yes, I remember a ragged young Egyptian was visiting the Museum Academy and he said to a friend that it ought to be called "Hadrian's goose-coop," because Caesar kept sending people there on fellowships and grants hoping they'd become poets and philosophers and so on, but all they gave him was lots of cackle and very few eggs. One of the Praetorian Guard overheard him and arrested him for disrespect and he was brought to Hadrian, but Hadrian burst out laughing and gave the young man a fellowship to spend a year at the Academy and shake them up! Then he gave the Praetorian a lacing for interfering with free speech.

But Aunt Bibi said to me afterwards the younger generation doesn't appreciate its advantages.

Strange and exciting, full of new noises and rare sights, odd smells and things I'd never seen before, and so many people—grown-up people; very few children were on the ships—sailing slowly up the ancient river Nile.

People were excited that Caesar's favorite attendant, Antinous, was coming on the trip. But he was grown-up too, about eighteen. Everyone said he was the most beautiful person in the world so I hoped I would have a chance to see him, anyway. Aunt Bibi said he was very kind and not a bit stuck-up about his looks or because he was Caesar's favorite page; still I felt I'd rather just see him from a distance as he would surely never notice me, a mere child.

Summer was coming on, the river was still rising and had become very wide at some points. The days were hot and damp but evening and night were almost always cool.

It was frightening at first to see the silvery moonlight forming strange little shiny circles on top of the water near the shore, because these were knobs on the backs of crocodiles and alligators as they rose to the surface, but they were quite far off and they never moved far from the riverbanks.

There were those flat, thick white flowers that lay on top of the water, too; some were deep gold, and they are very rich-looking and beautiful, but only native Egyptians could get them up, because they grew on great knots of thick smooth stems and you could easily get caught in them and never come up again, if you didn't carry a special knife and know how to slice through them.

Fuscus wasn't the only other young person on the imperial ship of the Empress Sabina, but he was the nearest my age, only a few years older, in fact.

I met him then for the first time, and it wasn't pleasant at all. I had escaped my maid and was exploring the ship as far as I could—I had to be careful not to be noticed or I'd have been snatched off to my own little section again. I think Aunt Bibi was taking a nap, and Aunt Chloe was somewhere else. So I climbed to the other side of the ship and I had crawled over some kind of rail and pushed through a double curtain behind which I'd heard young voices.

As soon as I got my head through I also got something else—something hard and round seemed to fly right at me, and at the same instant a hard shapeless something fell on me and bowled me over, and then before I had got my wits together again an angry face, with short straight blond hair around it, was glaring at me, and an irritated voice was shouting,

"What's the matter with you, you little idiot? Where the devil did *you* come from? You could have got yourself killed!"

And, getting up, this boy shook in my face a large round discus. "If I hadn't been close enough—!"

I saw then that he had quite a bruise, fresh and red, at the top of his arm, near the shoulder. I burst out crying.

"*I* get hit—and *she* cries!"

He was giving me that *boy* look, when they really despise a girl.

Some other boys now ran up; they were slaveboys; they took the discus away, one of them started putting salve on the bruise, which was beginning to turn bluish.

"Who are you, anyway?" He had calmed down a bit. "Where's your maid? What's your name?"

I still cried.

"Serves you right," he said, but not so angrily. "This is where I do my exercises—your people should have kept you out of here." Then, "What the devil are *you* crying for? This thing hurts—but it's hurting *me*, not you!"

"I'm . . . sorry," I bawled.

Then he couldn't help laughing.

"You do look funny. Whose daughter are you?"

I smoothed the tears off my face and tried to smooth my hair but it does get in such tangles.

"I'm Drusilla Vera Aureliana, daughter of the Augur—"

My breath caught and I didn't finish.

"Oh," he said, and I could see he was a bit impressed.

"I'm Cneius Pedanius Fuscus Salinator." He said it in a mixed way, a bit proud and a bit defensive; he knew, I suppose, that the Serviani weren't very popular, and that my father was a senator and head of a Sacred College of Augurs. And I noticed now the narrow stripe of purple along the edge of his chlamys, for a member of the imperial family. I

32

knew of course that his mother was Julia Aelia Serviana, the Emperor's niece, and that she had died. And when he didn't add "Junior" to his name, that reminded me his father had died too, and then I felt really terrible, thinking how awfully lonely he must be, and he so bravely hiding it.

But maybe he wasn't really feeling as bad as I had, in my time of trouble; I had been a whole lot younger when it happened to me, and maybe he hadn't felt about his father and mother the way I felt about mine.

"Well, anyhow, you shouldn't be in here," he said. "Go on back. You take her back." He nodded at one of the slaveboys, who came and stood behind me.

"Will you—will you—you won't tell my aunts?" I stammered.

"I'll tell the Emperor," he said, importantly.

"Oh—no—!"

"Will you promise to be good?"

"Good?"

"Always do everything I tell you?"

"I—I—don't know—"

"I—I—I'll ask my aunt," he mimicked. "Oh, get along with you. My grandfather will be coming in soon, and I want to practice discus some more."

So I went—but through the front of the little gym I noticed an old gentleman just about to go in. He glanced at me very curiously and muttered some-

33

thing to another man who was with him, and they both looked at me.

The first one as I ran past I recognized; *he* was old Senator Servianus, with a down of white hair around his mean, sharp face, and his eyes half-shut so that his glance looked like metal points that he was pinning you down with, and his lips were so tight crumpled-in you couldn't believe they ever opened.

I did notice that Fuscus resembled him rather, that his head had a sideward lean, in the same way, and he was thin in the same way, with longish hanging arms—but after I thought it over, I still liked Fuscus.

It was rather lonely for me on the ship and I pestered my aunts, I suppose. When I saw Fuscus again it was at a concert on the imperial deck of Caesar's ship, and he left his grandfather who was visiting near the Emperor, and came over to me. He was looking tanned and rather handsome, and he said, straightening his neck and shoulders in quite a manly way,

"Hello, young one. Why haven't you been coming to watch me practice discus?"

I was so thrilled, and so flabbergasted, I couldn't say anything. A big boy like that, really noticing me!

"Well—say something!"

"I—I—won't be in—the way?"

"Not if you take care. I'll have the boys keep an eye on you." He walked off, with big steps.

My heart really went pit-a-pat.

"Come along," said Aunt Bibiena. "Hetera's here to take you back and put you to bed." Hetera was my maid at that time; she was of the Roxolani race and had a name I couldn't pronounce so I called her Hetera. She was a thin girl who could stand still for hours in the same spot and never say a word she didn't have to; with that Roxolani language I don't blame her; they're real tongue-twisters.

So my aunts were glad to get rid of me an hour or two more, whenever one of Fuscus' servants came for me. It was really fun watching him throw; he had style, throwing a flat curve like at the Olympic games I once saw in Athens.

I guessed that he was lonely too; his face always brightened a bit when they brought me. Once he kissed my hand when I came; he played well that day and I told him he was very good and ought to win a prize. And once he told me that the great poet

Horace had written one of his odes to an ancestor of his called Fuscus, saying that if a man lived a pure and honest life he needn't fear anything, wolves would run away from him without harming him. (But a teacher told me that Horace was being satirical when he wrote that.)

Then one day he asked me—first he made the servants stand at a distance—if I thought him handsome.

I said Yes, when he kept his head straight; but he said he couldn't always, there was something wrong. I felt all warm and sorry for him then, and he looked rather like a baby when it doesn't know where its mother is, and well I kissed him and just then I felt an awful smack on the head and there was Aunt Bibiena as angry as a cat when you've stepped on its tail, and Fuscus laughed.

I must have looked funny then, but now that I think of it I don't believe he should have laughed.

Anyhow that was the last time I was permitted to see Fuscus on the trip, except when we met sometimes on shore; that was whenever we came to one of the Greek cities Alexander the Great had founded along the Nile five hundred years ago. Alexander had helped Greek veterans to settle there, and now of course their descendants were under Roman rule with Roman officials, and Hadrian naturally wanted to see how they were getting on.

They were all happy when he came because he

gave them new temples and libraries or restored old ones, and that gave a lot of new jobs, and he reformed the taxes and made sure the officials were behaving properly.

Only I didn't see Fuscus much because my maid never left me for a moment, and could that girl stick to you like a wet hair, even when I had to go, and here I was going to be eleven in ten months and a week! I thought it was truly humiliating, but did my aunts care how I felt about it? You can answer that yourself. Aunt Bibi is a good woman and I am fortunate that my father had a sister to take truly devoted care of me, but sometimes you can't help wishing she'd mind her own business more.

It made me miserable because I felt I really loved Fuscus and I was sure he was trying to see me more often. I told Aunt Bibiena I intended to complain to the Empress about the way my aunt distrusted me, but she gave me a look with her blue eyes bulging and I decided I had better not do that.

But Aunt Chloe was quite sweet; she stroked my hair and she promised she would bring me any message that Fuscus wanted to send. Nothing ever came, though; I suppose his mean old grandfather interfered on *his* end. Grown-ups are really awful to children, in many ways.

Because after all, Fuscus was more than fourteen and many boys of great families are engaged or even married by that age.

I suppose, now, that Servianus had higher aims for the Emperor's only direct heir, even though my father is one of the appointed patrician augurs, not the elected plebeians, and head of a Sacred College of Fifteen. And everyone knows the Aelii are colonial stock and not really patrician.

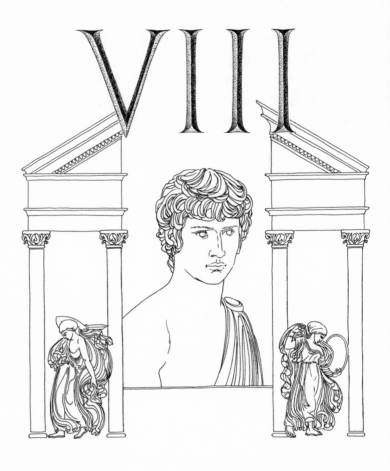

Yes, I could fear Hadrian, but I don't think he will
be angry at what I say . . . besides . . . I see those
great kind eyes of Antinous that at first seemed very
calm but when you looked a while longer you saw
there was something troubling him. And I remember the last words I ever heard him say.

It was strange about Antinous; he always seemed sad and thoughtful. I saw him often on the ship, usually whenever I went with my aunts attending the Empress Sabina at some afternoon musical or theatrical performance before the Emperor. I thought it curious the Emperor should like him better than the cheerful people who were always laughing and talking.

Yes, he seemed different from everybody. You would think him very fortunate, to be more beautiful than the greatest sculpture, and to be so favored by Caesar. But it didn't appear to make him happy.

Once I sat quite close to him. I was surprised when I looked up at him to see that he was looking at me instead of at the dancers who were performing. He smiled at me. I felt as though I were seeing the sun rise; he made you think of everything lovely. He had dark curling hair and soft dark eyes.

The afternoon was warm and slow music was being played, I remember, and he said to me, in that deep, gentle voice of his, "You're the only one who isn't falling asleep, Drusilla."

"I was listening to the music," I said.

He took my hand, and raised it to his lips, just as if I'd been a grown-up lady! Then he moved away, and a few minutes later he was saying something to Caesar, and Hadrian smiled too, and they both looked at me.

An attendant then came to me and took my hand and led me to Caesar.

"This is the little daughter of Drusus Verus, the augur," Caesar said. "It was Hermogenes who cured him of a strange illness." Then he spoke in another language for a while, and Antinous' face changed, he looked at me with such kindness and sympathy.

Somehow I began to feel rather unhappy, but Antinous said,

"Drusilla, you must never be afraid to come to Caesar if anything should ever trouble you. He will always find help for you."

"Your father is one of my friends, Drusilla," Caesar added.

And I must remember that.

Of course, this is not really to help father. And yet—in a way, it is, because the Senate is so opposed to what Caesar is doing. And perhaps—it may even help Caesar, in telling him something that may help him decide against an action which seems so unjust.

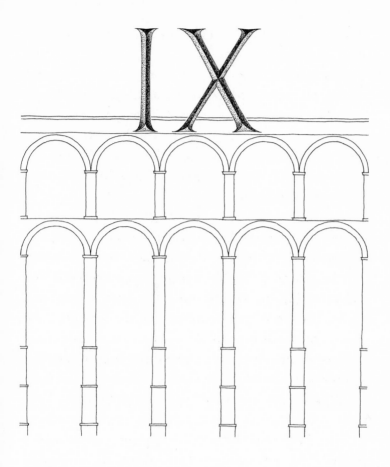

I know Aunt Bibi wouldn't want me to speak to
Caesar. She's a very serious woman, and thinks about
everything she plans to do until she decides not to
do it. She is still quite good-looking, but even when
she was younger, on the ship, she read books from
Caesar's traveling-library all the time. Aunt Chloe
seems a lot prettier because she has two maids just

for fussing with her looks, but Aunt Bibi won't do that. Father says Aunt Bibi is right and I should follow her example.

On the ship Aunt Chloe was always with some young man or with a crowd of people singing and laughing and talking about each other. She has red hair and keeps trying all those different kinds of dye to make it black. Sometimes it stays black so long that even I forget it's dyed.

But I took care not to forget really, because I could always make her do what I wanted by threatening to tell her new friends in the Greek cities that it was naturally red. She was nice to me anyway and would bring me sweets and cakes from the parties. Aunt Bibi took more care of me, though, only she wasn't as much fun; she belonged to a book-reading society of the Empress', and Sabina used to ask her opinions.

That doesn't mean she's right about Fuscus.

I sit here and the sun is deep and warm and I know I am safe and yet I am shivering as though I had just come out of bathing too long in a cold ocean.

I suppose I *am* really frightened at what I'm planning to do. But I couldn't go back now even if I decided to. You don't request an audience with the Emperor and then send your regrets that you can't come!

And now I remember perhaps the real reason why

I'm frightened—because I've seen Hadrian truly angry. And also I remember why I shouldn't be afraid.

It was when the ship put in at the city of Oxyrhynchos, the largest of the Greek city-colonies on the Nile. Rather, it had been the largest before that terrible flood.

I heard a lot of talk on the ship as we were coming toward the city about the flood. People remembered that Caesar had discussed it as far back as Alexandria, in the big Library Museum, with engineers and architects and finance experts, and they already knew that the Prytanis of Oxyrhynchos (they call it Oxy for short) was the man to blame; he had kept for himself—for years!—the tax money that was meant to be used for the cleaning-out of the canals and the maintenance and reinforcement of the dikes, and he had bribed the Nile inspectors to send false reports to the Praefect of Egypt. Aunt Chloe knew all this because the husband she had at that time was a designer for aqueducts, which are very important in Egypt.

And Aunt Chloe said that if there was one person on earth she wouldn't want to be it was a Greek named Kallikes (that was the Prytanis) when the Emperor got to Oxyrhynchos. She had never seen Hadrian *bleak* with rage the way he was in that chamber in Alexandria. He was going to try the case himself, he said, and all the gods in Olympos would not save Kallikes if he proved guilty.

45

So that was why we stopped so long in Oxy, although it was a frightful mess. Hadrian stayed in the palace of the Prytanis, whom he had had placed under guard with his family in a villa he owned; my aunts and I stayed with a Roman-born family, the Laberii; their father was Marius Laberius, and he had a son, young Marius; about a year after we were there they came back to Rome to live and they have the mansion next to ours.

They are darling people, and actually they are old friends, because Aunt Bibi had known the family in Rome before the elder Marius was appointed to Egypt. Aunt Chloe found out that young Marius' father and his uncle had both been in love with Aunt Bibi when they were young! Imagine—old Aunt Bibi! But of course she too was young, then. That was back in the year of Rome 870. She loved the uncle, but they quarreled; and then there came the uprising in Palestine and Cyrene, and he was called up for war, he was an officer, and he was killed at Cyrene. And by that time Marius was married, and young Marius was born. So Aunt Bibi didn't marry anybody.

The flood was so bad at Oxyrhynchos because the Nile has a delta here of nine little streams (that's why they call it Oxyrhynchos, which means Nine Snouts); the city is scattered all around these streams and then it rises to hills where all the better houses and the villas and mansions are.

So when it flooded ever so many people were drowned and there was tremendous damage in the lower part of the city; in fact it was almost swept away, being mostly wooden and papyrus, and on swampy-sandy ground.

Well, the trial began in the city hall of Oxy and there was the committee and the great Roman lawyer Salvius Julianus; he was one of the Imperial Council of Senators that usually went about with Caesar and he was helping codify Roman law; he hated doing it, but Hadrian made him.

So all morning Kallikes was getting along fine with Salvius questioning him hard and not catching him at all, he was quick and smug with all the answers, and Kallikes' wife was there; she was beautiful but in a heavy, ugly sort of way, hard-painted cheeks and a heap of dyed twisted black hair; her I saw when they opened the doors for someone to go in or out. Well naturally I wasn't in the courtroom but Aunt Bibi had brought me along and she had me wait in the corridor and I heard some of it and then there were my aunts and other people discussing it all very excitedly outside and they forgot I was listening; well that's the only way a child ever hears anything important.

Kallikes' wife was nodding at him and smiling in a stuck-up way, she said no Spanish-Roman soldier types were going to trap her wily Greek husband.

But then came the afternoon, and then Hadrian

himself began the cross-examination. And by and by —though Caesar spoke always quietly and simply— by and by Kallikes began stammering, and then recalling his words, and changing them, and adding things, and then turning red and then white. And then Hadrian asked him a most ordinary question it seemed—like what was the weather that day in Alexandria—and Kallikes turned absolutely yellow and couldn't breathe for a minute—and old Salvius Julianus simply gasped and then leaned toward another counselor and said in a loud whisper,

"And they call *me* the greatest cross-examiner in Rome! *He* is! I've always said so!"

Anyhow pretty soon Kallikes began crying and confessing everything! how he had known that the dikes had been choking up for years, and sand-and-mud islands were forming in the canals, and every season at the rising of the Nile when the Nilometers registered higher and higher, he told the people who were worried that it only meant a bigger harvest than ever. And as for himself and his wealthy friends, he knew that if a flood came *they* would be all right because their estates were on higher land and their mansions were stone and marble.

Well, then Hadrian suddenly stood up and the whole court with him, he couldn't stand it any more, and he then and there sentenced Kallikes to be crucified—that's the usual punishment for colonial officials who steal public funds and give the Roman rule a bad name.

That woman Kallikes' wife began to scream and guards kept her away by force while Hadrian and the court went out of the Curia, but in the corridor she got hold of Antinous, who for some reason was one of the last to leave, and she threw herself down on the floor and grabbed him by the feet and was kissing his sandals and promising him all her most beautiful ancient statues if he would only ask Caesar to save Kallikes' life.

A lot of her friends were there and they had brought Kallikes' little boy all dressed in black and bawling, and they pushed him into Antinous' arms and begged,

"Save his father! pity the innocent child!"

Antinous was disgusted because you could see he was thinking of the drowned fathers, but he was sorry for the baby and he gave it back gently to its nurse and he stepped away from Kallikes' wife and said in that beautiful slow deep voice of his that there could be no appeal from Caesar's justice.

Caesar had heard it all and he turned and stopped and let them all come close to him except that the guards kept the wife of Kallikes down on the floor and gripped her arms over her head. And he said quite harshly,

"Tell this woman that when her husband brings me back the people who died in his flood, I will revoke his sentence."

Then the woman howled "Tyrant!" and then, "I will have all my statues burned!" because she knew

49

how Hadrian loves ancient Greek art and she had two by Phidias, the greatest sculptor of all. Antinous looked shocked and he bit his lip. Hadrian's eyes really flashed lightning and he said, but calmly,

"I confiscate all your property in the name of the Senate and the Roman people. It will be sold for the benefit of the sufferers," and he went out of the building and the rest followed him and I heard people wildly cheering him outside.

Fuscus was there in the court and I don't think he saw me at all, and he came out with some important official of Oxy (Servianus wasn't there) and I heard him say as they passed me,

"Well, now you see why the Roman Senate hates Hadrian." But the man gave him a sort of ugly little grin and Fuscus didn't say any more.

I knew even then that the Senate often opposed Caesar, yet I was surprised that a Roman boy should say a thing like that to a provincial. Still, older people often say things that make you wonder why . . .

I would truly fear to make Hadrian angry. I do know how great he is. I know he would not spare anyone who might trouble Rome.

But Fuscus is innocent. He is not a troubler.

Some more of Caesar's Praetorian Guard went by now, at a marching-step, with their metal breast-plates and metal-spaced tunics and spears, and a tall, strong-looking man, black but not an Egyptian; I could tell he came from central Africa; he was deep black and his features were more gentle than the Egyptian men's. He noticed me and he smiled.

"What's this little rose-flower doing here?" he said.

My Aunt Bibiena had come out of the courtroom now and she knew him, it seemed.

"I have caught you, Florus!" she laughed. "Now you must come and read your new poems to the Empress' literary club, this very afternoon."

"But it was arranged to take place in the palace of the Prytanis," he answered, looking really caught. "That surely isn't being used now?"

"Why not? No, Florus, you won't escape."

He made a face. Then he bent down, picked me up as if I were a straw, and swung me onto his shoulder. "Tell me your name."

"Put me down first!" I was scared to be so high.

"But I couldn't hear you talk, when my ears are all the way up here, and your mouth is all the way down there!"

Aunt Bibi was smiling, so I told him.

"I am Drusilla Vera Aureliana."

He looked serious and put me down carefully.

"Ah, you are a very important little lady!"

"She is my niece, Florus, daughter of Lucius Drusus, senator and augur at Rome. Drusilla, this is Florus Africanus, a great poet. He writes in Latin, so you will soon be learning some of his verses."

"I will make a bargain with you, Lady Bibiena," Florus said. "I will use this afternoon to write an ode to this little charmer"—he meant *me!*—"and in

return you will make my excuses to the Empress'
ladies."

Aunt Bibi shook her head scoldingly but she
smiled.

"Very well. It's a bargain."

"Are you going to tell a lie, Aunt Bibi?" I was
curious about it because she always told me not to.

"Of course not—it won't be a lie if Florus keeps
his word! I intend to tell them he is writing an ode."

"You won't say in the poem that my hair is red?"
I asked him. Florus bent far down, pretending to cup
his ear in order to hear me; he was really very tall.
Then he frowned, pretending to be surprised.

"I told you I couldn't hear what you said. You
didn't say anything about *red* hair?"

"Yes. Red." He wrinkled his short nose, hard.

"I don't *see* anybody here with red hair. All I see
is a very young lady with curly sunshine all around
her head."

I suppose I smiled very happily at that. My aunt
really couldn't help laughing.

"You *are* a young rascal, Florus! Remember, now
—an ode to my Drusilla. And please remember, I
don't want to have to wash out her mouth when she
recites it!"

Florus winked and smiled. Florus wasn't young, he
had a curly beard. He went off quickly now, scratch-
ing his head as if he were wondering how he was
going to do what he promised.

I'm pretty sure he did write it and he did give it to Aunt Bibi because I saw once in her room a set of verses on a wax tablet, but I hardly managed to see the first line, "Some day every rose shall bloom" —when she came in and grabbed it away from me and locked it up in a drawer.

"But, Aunty," I said, "it's only about roses."

"You'll see it when you're older," she said.

Well I haven't seen it yet.

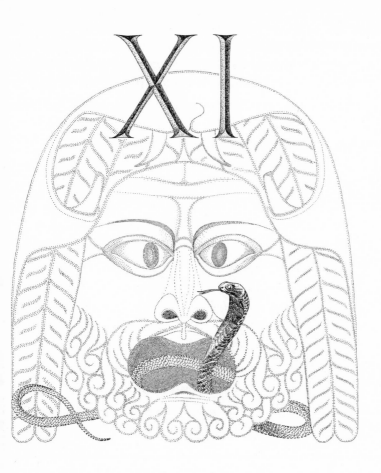

I clearly remember one morning.

We were passing through a very horrid place on the Nile, where the mists were so thick you could hardly see across to the shores of the river even if you wanted to, but there was nothing to see along there, just long low lines fuzzy with distant palm trees.

And the insects were awful—hordes of tiny things that you couldn't see or beat away; everybody had to be wrapped in gauze veiling, all but our hands. It didn't last more than a day or two, else I think nobody would ever have traveled past that point in the river.

But in the meantime you couldn't see much and you couldn't even hear people very distinctly when they talked.

I was so bored that I went anywhere I could creep, all over the ship. And at one place, on the upper deck, I heard voices, and very clearly.

"Nimini-piminy! Namby-pamby!" a voice was jeering. It was an old voice, an old man's. "You think you will ever get anywhere *that* way?" I thought I knew that voice.

"Why must I get anywhere?" the other voice whined, and it was a young voice. "You're always plaguing me I must look forward to becoming Emperor, when you *know* I don't want to be! It's nothing but worries and solemn old fogies round you and stuffy old meetings! I want to have good times—"

"Parties, girls! you think that will make you happy! You forget you're next of kin to Hadrian; you will have no peace after he dies unless you *are* Emperor. You will be persecuted, suspected, by whoever else may become Caesar. He'll always think you plotting against him, to take his throne. Your life won't be worth a brass coin. That boy of Caesar's is only the first one you've got to put out of your way."

"But why should anybody bother me if I don't *want* to be Caesar, if I refuse to be?"

"Because nobody will believe you. It's kill or be killed. . . . Oh, don't start crying again!"

"I know what you're going to say now, and I won't have it, Grandfather! I've told you again and again, and I do mean it. I like him—he's never made any trouble!"

Servianus' voice was thick with despising Fuscus.

"You ninny! You *like* him—you don't want to be Emperor! D'you think *he* wouldn't put *you* to death if Hadrian makes him his heir?"

"But how could he? That boy—he's nobody—!"

Servianus snapped back.

"Enough of that! He is *not* nobody."

"Nobody knows where he came from, even!"

"*You* don't know, yet. But *I* know. Emperor Hadrian knows."

"Everybody knows that Caesar keeps him around because he is the handsomest boy in the world—and very intelligent—but that's not enough to make him heir—"

"No, it is not enough; it wouldn't matter at all, only he's a great deal more than that."

"You don't even *tell* me," Fuscus exclaimed.

"I'll tell you—afterwards."

"There isn't going to be any afterwards because I'm not going to—to talk to the oarsm—"

The word "oarsman" was snapped off before Fuscus could finish it, just as if someone had shoved something into his mouth.

"You haven't the discretion of a monkey!" Servianus said. "I heard something moving quite near us—"

So I slipped away, and they never noticed.

I hadn't really meant to eavesdrop. I'm not that kind. I hadn't known anyone was there.

But I knew whom they were talking about.

May the gods forgive me, I knew whom they were talking about. If only I had spoken to my aunt!

But I was very young. A child may be well able to understand the words older people say, yet not understand the meaning, nor even whether they do mean it or not.

So often a child is laughed at, or not regarded at all. People believe that a child is truthful—or unable to know how to construct a lie, and I think this is so; yet they often won't believe a child.

I thought about what I had heard, and I worried about it, but how could I understand what it really meant? And I didn't know whom to talk to. My aunt Bibiena was far too busy with her plans for getting into the service of the Empress; she hoped for a permanent place at the court when we got back to Rome; and my aunt Chloe was in love with some important man and never listened when I spoke to her.

Besides, I couldn't believe it because it seemed impossible that anybody should want to harm *him*.

And then, one morning, suddenly, terribly . . .

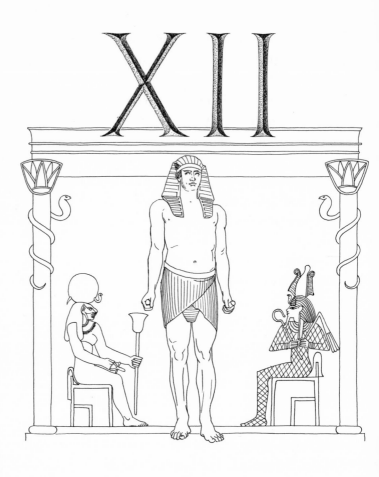

I *can't* tell how it happened, because I don't *know!* When you're waked up at dawn by all kinds of screaming and shouting, and people come streaming down onto the deck where you're in your little room sleeping with the curtain parted—and some of them are pale as ghosts and others are scarlet with shock and everybody is choking or crying or saying,

"O Zeus," and Aunt Bibiena comes tearing up to you, her eyes staring wide and her curls all loose from being put on too fast—and your aunt Chloe rushes in all frowsy and blowsy and still holding a man by the hand whom you never saw before—

All Aunt Bibiena said when she grabbed me and kissed me a dozen times on the forehead, she said, "Oh, it was his *son*—his *son*—but don't tell anybody, be sure you don't tell anybody—"

Can you wonder I have never really known how it happened, only that it *happened?*

"*Who* was *whose* son?" I demanded, but Aunt Bibiena ran out again; on the way she stopped and slapped Aunt Chloe hard—Chloe is much younger —and said "You little slut! get rid of that fellow"— and she vanished.

"Aunt Chloe, who was *whose* son?" I said again, catching at her clothes, but she pulled them close and snapped, "O let me be" and she ran out too.

I called my maid who was standing at the door shaking and crying.

"What happened? For heaven's sake!"

But she only cried louder, and then I jumped out and I pulled her arm.

"Tell me! if you don't tell me I'm going to beat you so hard you'll drop dead!"

Then she cried, "Oh, domina, domina—he is dead —he was so kind to us all—Caesar will put us all to death—all the slaves—"

Finally I got it out of her. That dear, beautiful

Antinous—he had been carried up out of the river, drowned!

No one seemed to know how.

In the dreadful days that followed, the whole line of Roman galleys lay still, rocking on the slow tide; Caesar's deck was completely closed off, we heard only whispers, and the ship of the Empress Sabina was turned about and sent to the end of the line— why? what had *we* to do with it?—and we stayed in the marina of the Greek city we had last visited, without moving forward or backward. It was a long time before people at last began talking naturally again.

I tried to find out where Fuscus was. They only told me that he was sick, and had been taken to the ship where the physician Hermogenes was residing. I never asked about Servianus; it seemed nobody was talking to him. I just wished *he* had been drowned, instead.

One thing I still wonder: why had Hadrian ever let Servianus come along on the trip? Yes, he was one of the Imperial Council that usually accompanied the Emperor, but it was Hadrian who had started this council and he picked its members and couldn't he have left Servianus behind? Or maybe he knew he couldn't trust him and thought it was safer to keep him under his own eyes. But a really good person like Hadrian can never figure out what a real snake will do.

As for Caesar himself—he had shut himself away as much as humanly possible. Only his most trusted attendant, Mastor, a former soldier of the wild Jazyges tribe, was with him. The body of Antinous had been washed with some kind of preservative balm that an Egyptian priest had brought and said it would last forever if not exposed to the air—and so Antinous was kept secretly put away; afterward Hadrian built a whole new little city on the Nile and called it after him.

They said Antinous had fallen into the river and that an oarsman had jumped in to save him, then another oarsman, but only the second oarsman had come up alive.

I heard people saying that Hadrian was going to cut the whole trip short and give up trying to find the sources of the Nile and go home. But then at last the ships began to sail again; I watched the current and saw that we were going on up the river.

It rather surprised me when, after another week or so, our ship, the ship of the Empress Sabina, was turned completely around and we headed back down the Nile, going home.

And the way I felt about it—tremendously glad —I knew I'd been homesick a long time. I was only sorry because of that rather nice boy Marius I'd met at Oxy. But Fuscus was going home, too, so I didn't mind much about Marius.

But it is utterly clear that Fuscus had nothing

to do with the tricks and plots of Servianus! This terrible tragedy was not his work. This I know myself and I shall prove to Caesar that Fuscus is innocent. Servianus is the only villain, and none but Servianus should be made to pay for it!

So we came home to Rome and it was so happy to be back with father again and my friends and my pet parrot and my goldfish, but there were too many of them in the pool now, we had to strain some of them out and I gave them to my maid and that barbarian threw them into the garbage.

I didn't hear anything from Fuscus for a long time, but I knew he'd been sick on the boat and wouldn't talk to anybody on the journey home. I felt terrible too, whenever I thought of what had happened to Antinous.

Staunch Aunt Chloe! She was a real friend.

If there's one thing in life that makes all troubles worthwhile to her, it is romance.

Instead of scaring me away from the possible wiles of Fuscus, he was then in his mid-teens, she eagerly cooperated. If he gave her a message for me, she'd hide it in her hair till she saw me; if she saw him at a court affair, she'd tell me she was sure he missed me—but how could she know that? She would hint that she knew when he was going to be present at the next public athletic games, and she would see to it that I should come with her and her current husband (did I mention that she had been married and divorced again and now she was on her fourth try).

I can't say really why, and yet no matter what happens, I still feel that Fuscus is somehow very close to me, and that I must help him all I can. Any other boy might become awfully annoyed with a child like me caring about him, but Fuscus never seems to.

Of course he has girl friends, and I do feel jealous when I hear about them, for they have one advantage I can never hope to beat them at, they are his age or a bit older; he seems to choose them older. But we've never been allowed to see each other for more than a few minutes at a time, anyway, and always in the presence of other people!

Fuscus was sent to school, just like Marius and Annius Verus, though he was of Imperial and Senatorial rank. Servianus wanted him to mix and to learn to be popular.

This is hard for Fuscus; he is very shy, and only at ease, I suppose, with me; he used to show off to me, because I was so young that I was always awed by anything he knew or could do, in study, or games, or tootling on a flute, which he wasn't allowed to do in Servianus' home, where of course he lived.

But he would do things I hated, that made me feel ashamed of him, like when he unmercifully beat a slaveboy who couldn't help grinning when Fuscus sang off-key in front of me; he flew at him and beat him. I couldn't stand that.

Still, it's rather hard for a person when he can't do anything really well.

Marius, on the other hand, does everything well.

Why shouldn't he? There's nothing at all to worry him. His family practically escaped any real loss from the Oxy flood, they're settled in a beautiful house adjoining ours, not far from the Palatine Hill, and Aunt Bibi adores him; she says he is the image of his uncle, with his large, blue, sparkly eyes, his tall, broad-shouldered figure, and his kind ways.

But he does worry about one thing, he tells me, and that is how I can possibly care about Fuscus.

"All the philosophers tell us," he said once, when

we were walking in his garden, "that the only thing men really know about women is that men can never know them. Of all the boys you've met, why Fuscus? He's plain, he's not bright, I doubt if he's much interested in you—and yet—!"

"I'm not in love with him, if that's what you're asking, Marius."

"I wasn't asking," he took me up quickly, "so I wonder why you answer."

I said nothing to that, and he went on.

"If I thought you were, I'd surely tell your father."

"Why? Couldn't *I* tell him—but you know there is nothing serious!"

No, I was sure there was nothing serious. Yet I am so fond of Fuscus. Perhaps it's just because he seems to have so much, yet really has so little.

"Why would you tell my father?" I asked.

"Because Fuscus will do you no good!" he burst out. "Don't think it is only because I—because I care about you, that I say this. I would warn any girl about Fuscus. He's been spoiled rotten by his grandfather and by people who value him for his rank and his riches. And I know it is *not* for these things that you care. So I—well, I wonder about it."

"You don't understand Fuscus. He's a very unhappy boy. You don't understand what it means to have nobody who really cares for you."

Marius said no more at this time. He simply went on to tell me about his new tutors, his friends at the

Academy, his father's new business ventures; he laughed about his young sister's desire to become a Vestal Virgin—"she thinks her heart is broken about some boy whose name she'll have forgotten by next week." And I told him the same sort of thing about myself, my studies, my visits.

I quarreled with him next time because right after I told him how Fuscus couldn't carry a tune (I didn't tell how Fuscus beat the slaveboy because that seemed like tattling) we were walking in Marius' garden and we sat down on a bench and after a while Marius began singing, very softly. He had turned his head away and didn't seem to be meaning me to hear. It was a perfectly beautiful little duet of Horace's, that famous one, "While you found me very pleasing"—fifty composers must have put it to music, though it's not really a love song—well, he was singing it, and his voice was, oh, not so very beautiful, but somehow you loved it, it gave you a little shiver, it was so—it came so close to you, I don't know how to describe it.

And it made me angry, as though he were trying to take advantage of Fuscus, because it was really difficult to sing, it had so many turns where you could lose the tune, but Marius sang it as true as a bird. And it seemed to me it wasn't fair.

There is something about injustice that makes me wild! I cannot bear it, especially in people I like.

And so I *must* tell Caesar what I know.

XIV

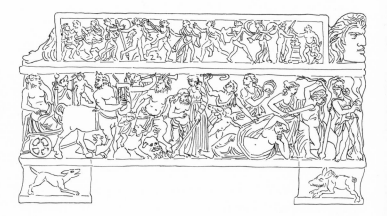

This past summer things have been pretty touchy around our house. Aunt Chloe has been running about making a hundred plans for the parties, festivals, games, and whatever that were coming along. This year her hair has to be brown, which is her current husband's preference.

All this because it is the year of Rome 890, which is nothing, but it's the twentieth anniversary of Emperor Hadrian's reign, which is everything!

Aunt Bibiena made me write a festival essay about the Emperor which she has had engraved—she thinks I'm going to be a writer, ha ha! She planned to have me read it at the big banquet that Caesar gave for almost everybody, but who had time to bother with anything like that? Besides, I never finished it really.

All Rome will be at that banquet! Even the slaves get a special Saturnalia, and hordes of them will be in the Campus Martius. They really have reason to celebrate Hadrian's rule; he's the first—Aunt Bibi says so and she's making me study it up—the first emperor that ever made laws giving the slaves any rights. And when Hadrian makes a law, he means business.

I just hope he knows what he's doing, but when you see a society lady banished for mistreating her maids, and a master jailed because a slave died after a beating, and no private slave-prisons permitted any more—well, it makes you think. Already a maid talked back to Aunt Chloe when she slapped her for dropping an ivory-framed silver mirror, and where is *that* going to end up?

. . . No. I'm ashamed of what I just said. Caesar is perfectly right. I ought to take it back. But Annius Verus would say that I was being insincere; we shouldn't be ashamed to make mistakes, only of not correcting them. Still, Annius Verus *is* a prig, sometimes. He and Marius have the same tutor, Fronto. Annius simply worships Fronto, who is certainly very clever. But Marius thinks Fronto's rather a bore, he gets angry over so many things. Marius wishes Annius Verus wouldn't be quite so philosophical; he *never* gets angry. He sleeps on a bare pallet, on the *floor!*

The great triumphal arch near the Colosseum has been repaired and they're putting up a set of magnificent plaques, four on each side, I believe. Last time I went with Aunt Bibiena to the Palatine, I saw some of the designs in the sculptor's workshop there. There is more of Antinous in those plaques than of Caesar, considering that it's supposed to be in honor of Caesar. There's Antinous in the group with Caesar as he leaves Rome; there's Antinous at the famous boar hunt. There's Antinous at the other famous hunt, when Hadrian hunted a huge man-eating lion and killed it with a spear flung down its throat. And then there's a sacrifice to a young god who looks more like Antinous than like Apollo. Making him a god seems to some people a bit too much for someone who wasn't of the emperor's own family. But, after all, who is to judge?

To think of that brute Servianus . . .

Now I recall it, I saw a large bust of the Empress Plotina, Trajan's wife—and somehow the face reminded me of somebody else. Plotina seems a very handsome woman—you wouldn't call her pretty, but such fine, classic features. Who is it I recall as being so much like her?

There was quite a row at home, because Fuscus sent a message asking to take me to the great festival banquet. It had to be a formal request, of course, made to father and Aunt Bibiena, who takes care of the household. Father said no, positively. Aunt Chloe said,

"But Fuscus could seat Drusilla at Caesar's own table!"

Father said it didn't matter; I could go with *him* and sit with him in the Vestal Virgins' box, which is his privilege as head of a Sacred College of Augurs. Who wants to sit with those old maids, asked Aunt Chloe, which was pretty awful of her. And that settled it; father sent a reply to Fuscus that I would be with the Vestals.

Now what had Fuscus done this time that was wrong?

Marius was sulky about it because he had planned to take me, and now Fuscus had spoiled it all. But was that Fuscus' fault?

Aunt Bibi did come to the festival banquet; we almost thought she wouldn't, she had been so depressed since last year when the Empress Sabina died. I don't think most people cared much; the

Lady Sabina was a cold, proud woman; she was the grandniece of Trajan, and she never liked Trajan's wife, Plotina; she sometimes hinted to her friends that not all the truth was known about Plotina, whom everybody revered so much. And she was perfectly hateful to that dear Antinous who never did her any harm—never did anybody any harm.

I had to go to the interment of the Empress; I didn't want to but Aunt Bibi made me; she said I was a young lady now and I couldn't stay away from public ceremonies just because I didn't like going, especially because I was daughter of a head Augur. It was pouring rain all the time but the whole procession had to go winding in and out of all those terraces and ramps of the new Mausoleum, and down to the gloomy lower chambers that were like dungeons. I believe the ashes of the Emperor's father and mother were already buried there, and some other important people.

I didn't see Hadrian close on this occasion because of all the others who were there, and his face was veiled a lot of the time because he was officiating as Pontifex Maximus and the ceremonials sometimes required it. But he looked terrible, his face had a grayish-yellow color and his eyes were dull; his left arm shook sometimes, and now and then he seemed to forget to finish what he was saying. I couldn't help being afraid he was ill.

It was truly gruesome and I was never so happy as when we got out of the Mausoleum and into the

74

open, away from all those deep crypts and passages. From outside, the building was all sparkling bright white marble, with circles of statues all around and statues along the marble bridge, but there are gloomy pines and dark green cypresses all around the peaked top. Hadrian designs all his buildings *round*.

The arrangements for the festival banquet were changed again! Father couldn't take me. So I was escorted by Annius Verus and reclined at a table near Caesar, with about fifty other "personages," if you please! I was hoping when the imperial family messenger came that perhaps Fuscus had managed it after all for him and me to go together, but no such luck.

I missed him and I wanted to see how he was; he had been looking quite pale, and thinner than usual. Why didn't he *do* something to get away from the household of his grandfather? I'm sure Caesar would have liked him better by himself, and would have trusted him more if he hadn't been so tied up with that conspiring old family enemy of the Aelii. How could an Aelius like Hadrian be friendly with a Servianus, who's always done everything he could to make trouble, and marrying Hadrian's sister, just to be close enough to spite him without Hadrian being able to hit back? But he never got nearer to being emperor, and he's past ninety years old now—imagine it! And still spry!

I told Annius Verus, on the way to the festival

banquet, when our chariot couldn't get through the solid crush of people trying to reach the Palatine hill and the Colosseum and the Campus Martius, that I didn't know why he had asked me.

"Well, I didn't really want to," he said, with that earnest look of his gray eyes. "Lady Faustina wanted me to bring *her,* but, after all, friendship has its duties."

"Duties! Do you think it's a duty, taking me? I'm not as pretty as Lady Faustina, but—"

"It's not a question of prettiness; I'm supposed to marry Faustina, you know, some day. It's arranged. Her family are very sure that Caesar plans to adopt me—"

"Make *you* his heir? Then you are to be emperor? You, so young?"

"Not while I'm young; there is to be—someone else before me." Annius Verus was remembering that he ought to be more discreet, even with an augur's daughter. "It looks as though Caesar might be planning a new sort of Triumvirate, a kind of Council of Three to share the imperial power—one for executive rule and leadership, one for cultural growth, literature, art, aesthetics—and a younger one who will grow up to take the place of the executive. He wants to prevent one-man rule."

"My father told me Caesar sent the Senate a list of twelve names of worthy men," I said, "to ask them which one they would believe best to succeed

76

him as emperor. It rather frightened me; is he really that ill?"

"We must not expect the impossible; no one is immortal." Annius looked very serious.

I couldn't bear the thought any more. "I still don't see why taking me was a duty!" and I laughed. "Come—who asked you to?"

"Well, Marius asked me. He wanted to make sure Fuscus wasn't organizing a trick to have you sit with *him*."

I thought, no wonder Caesar called Annius "Verissimus," most true, instead of "Verus," true. It will be strange if that young man ever develops any diplomacy!

I've never seen a banquet chamber so gloriously decorated! The marble pillars were all wreathed with roses up to their huge capitals and seemed rising into the very ceiling; they'd been freshly painted with pictures of rosy clouds and the gods and goddesses looking down smiling. Singing birds flew about, gorgeous-colored peacocks and parrots nested in the green bushes ranged along the marble walls, dipping their bright heads into the fountains that tossed sparkling sprays into the air. Veils of rose petals drifted downward constantly. Soft music played, and everywhere were the golden signs, "*Sic Decem, Sic Viginti.*"

I never saw so many couches and so many dining-tables and so many hundreds of guests—and the elder women with such hair-do's, so high and so elaborate, done with gold and jewels and arrangements like miniature buildings! some even had butterflies or cages with tiny live birds netted somehow, with gold wire I suppose, into their hair.

Aunt Bibi was quite disgusted; she said the lady Sabina would never have approved of all this, and the necklines of the women! they simply weren't *neck*lines.

"They're like ships' loading-lines," grinned Marius. That boy had done a job worthy of the crafty Ulysses himself—with Annius Verus' cooperation, of course, though I think Annius was a "silent partner" and didn't know what it was all about. Marius had got himself into our company and on to the other side of me at the festival by the simple process of escorting Aunt Bibiena!

I suppose Aunt Bibi saw through the game quite well, and that must have been why she came, because she loves Marius and loathes Fuscus.

The music began and then everybody stood up with a loud cry and the music suddenly tripled and became very joyous, as the imperial party entered and came up to the great table where the ivory-and-gold couch of the Emperor stood, on the dais. We were quite near it though our seats were not at the same table.

Caesar looked truly splendid, not because of the purple toga and all the gold, and the gold wreath on his great bull-like forehead, but he appeared so stately and cordial. The senators sat all around him, the augurs and the military chiefs nearby, and the other important people. Just once, for a moment, I thought he had that sick, gray look—it gave me a little shock of terror—but then I saw it was only the shadow of a torchlight.

The Empress Sabina having died only about a year before, the seat at Hadrian's right hand was empty. But I noticed that there was no seat at all at his left—and I remembered then that this is where Antinous would have been sitting if he had lived. There was always something special in the way Caesar regarded him; narrow-minded petty people said it was only because of his classic good looks, but if so, why didn't Caesar replace him after his death? He has built a new city on the Nile and named it after Antinous, and he has decreed Antinous to be a god, the way members of the imperial family are supposed to become gods after they die.

He has never done anything without good reason; there *must* have been some cause for all that.

It makes me feel sad to remember that dear person. But it was such a bright and wonderful evening!

Everyone was so exalted and so merry; Caesar drank and passed his gold cup around to everybody. Even that nasty old Servianus was sitting there and smiling, and I was glad to see Fuscus looking well and almost cheerful, on the couch next to his. Fuscus smiled and waved to me—he had had a few bumpers of wine and was rather flushed; I did not wave back, of course; Aunt Bibi was watching me like mad. He had a new girl with him, dark, the prettiest thing I ever saw, but horridly made-up.

The food was superb, of course, and in the midst of the celebrating and merry-making, Hadrian did as he has the habit of doing—suddenly called for food from the furthest tables of the most insignificant guests, and tasted some of it himself, because he wanted to make sure no one was being served inferior quality. It was good, naturally, because the cooks knew they might be tested, and they weren't taking any risks.

After the meal, dancers came in and they were from all the different provinces of the empire, except Judea where there was still trouble. One dancer slipped in a wine-puddle that some careless people had made with their libation to the gods, pouring it on the marble floor instead of into the bowls provided; he had to be carried out, but Caesar sent him a little purse of gold so I daresay the others wished they had slipped, too!

But the best of all, to me, was when the prize for the finest ode in praise of Caesar was awarded. And I saw a huge, black, graceful figure rise up, smiling radiantly, and go toward Caesar's couch—and it was Florus Africanus, that darling man who had been so kind to me when I was a child at the city of Oxyrhynchos on the Nile, and he wrote me that ode which Aunt Bibi won't let me see.

It turned out that Caesar had changed the subject for the prize poem; he had said he didn't want anything that would cause forced flatteries to be written. He had left the subject open, and now—guess what! Florus had won the contest with a poem on springtime!

So now Florus sat up there—on the dais!—and he took out his manuscript and he read it aloud. I am sure he saw me and remembered me because at one line he stopped and smiled right at me and waved his arm! But maybe it was Aunt Bibi he recognized and was waving to.

This is how it began—Florus' voice was rich and warm and yet very distinct—he called it "The Vigil of Venus."

> Who never loved, when dawns tomorrow shall be
>   caught by love's sweet chain,
> And he who loved, when dawns tomorrow shall return
>   to love again;

Springtime new, the world renewing, brings the
dancing and the song,
Springtime brings love's bright harmonic, weds the
birds and weds the throng . . .
Who never loved, when dawns tomorrow shall be
caught by love's sweet chain,
And he who loved, when dawns tomorrow shall return
to love again.

And so it went on, beautifully, all the way to the
end, every verse ending in those two first lines.

Soft music was playing all the time, and when it
was over—I think we were all a bit hazy with the
wine and the music and the excitement—Florus
came up to Caesar and received from his own hand
the prize, which was Hadrian's own gold cup! And
then Hadrian said something to Florus that made
him burst into tears—but tears of joy!

It came out that Florus had been exiled long ago
—I think by Trajan, or maybe Domitian—because
the Roman-born poets were jealous of him. And in
his last verse of this poem Florus pleads to be let
stay in Rome, and now Hadrian has granted him
Roman residence, and has awarded him a little
house!

Right at the end came the speeches. They were
short, and of course all of them in praise of Caesar;
there were one or two senators, and Servianus, that
old hypocrite, who spoke. Then some of the top experts in their professions praised Caesar's talents,
an architect spoke of his architectural work—as a

matter of fact they didn't always praise him; this architect said the Pantheon though grand and of inspired new style showed some touches of the amateur, like the clumsy joining of the old portico with the new rotunda—Hadrian wasn't a bit angry, he just interrupted, "Why didn't you tell me *then?*" But the architect only grinned and went on. And Salvius Julianus told how Caesar wouldn't let him make a living till he had codified the law—everyone burst out laughing because Salvius is almost the richest lawyer in Rome!

And so it went till Caesar got up himself—and then the banqueting hall really rocked with everyone roaring *"Ave Caesar!"* and all sorts of congratulations and mostly *"Sic Decem, Sic Viginti"*—As for ten years, so for twenty—and then they were quiet, and Caesar spoke.

It was only a few words . . . but what words . . .

It was so moving—and suddenly I realized—maybe everyone did—that he knew there would not be very much more time for him to be Emperor. I can't remember a word of it, only that when he finished, I had one hand in Aunt Bibi's hand and the other in Marius' hand, and I was holding on to them tight, and nobody even breathed.

And then in the deep quiet, he said more. He said,

"I have called a special meeting of the Senate for tomorrow afternoon. I shall then make an—important—announcement."

People gasped, and stared at each other.

Hadrian was looking directly, with a solemn, kindly look and the least little smile—looking directly and unmistakably at Titus Antoninus; Antoninus always looks serious anyway but then his face grew tense and he reddened; then Caesar looked at Annius Verus, who slowly bowed his head and looked as if he might weep.

But Servianus! His almost bald head began to quake as if he had a sudden palsy. And Fuscus—he looked as if all his features had suddenly fallen out of place.

But somehow the mood of happiness didn't change—I suppose we were all swept away with the whole feeling of the evening—and after all, Caesar might live another ten years—so our hopes were all up and it was a wonderful evening for everyone, and it seemed that nothing at all had happened to mar it.

Until I came home.

It was too, too dreadful.

It is certainly no mistake for Caesar to get rid of Servianus, no matter what the Senate thinks. Hasn't he pestered the world long enough? I begin to understand that old harpy the Empress Livia, Augustus' wife . . . she simply poisoned people like him.

Oh, I mustn't think that way.

Isn't it strange, how evil people actually make you become like themselves—make you want to do the kind of thing *they* do, so that you feel you're just as bad as they are at heart, and then you wonder if they are *really* bad, since you can have the same feelings, and yet you know *your* intentions are good . . .

Oh, that Annius Verus! His philosophizing gets hold of me sometimes! I'm glad I'm not his Faustina; I'd be bored to death.

This is what happened:

Annius Verus had brought me home, my head quite turned and full of glory and happiness and that great Greek wine and the vast final cry of the crowds, *"Sic Decem, Sic Viginti!"* and the fulfilled look on the face of Hadrian, who deserves everything good from his Rome. . . . And I was getting ready for bed, when Aunt Chloe came in very excited and told my maid to go; she was falling asleep anyway and no use in undressing me.

Aunt Chloe was looking very pretty, her curls quite brown and you could hardly tell that her face had that new hard make-up paste on.

"He's *here,*" she whispered.

"Here?" I was flustered cold. "You mean—?"

"Your future"—she merely mouthed the next word. *"Be clever.* I'll help."

She gave me a push, and there I was through the door and onto the balcony, among the potted trees.

For the moment I couldn't think of anything but

what Annius Verus had told me in the chariot, and I was almost startled wondering how Chloe had changed from being on Fuscus' side to Annius' side —it must have been all the wine and the poem and the excitement—but when I saw *Fuscus* standing there, in the plain tunic of an ordinary citizen— the moonlight made him very clear—I was utterly dumb.

"Drusilla!" He was looking miserable and frightened, not at all loverlike. "I've got to tell you something—ask you—it's important—and secret . . ."

He had that vexed, puzzled expression, knitting his brows, biting his lips, that makes him look like a little boy, coming to me because his mother was nowhere to be found. And it *almost* always turns me into putty. But not *always*.

"What is it, Fus—" But I quickly recalled that I should not speak his name, if it was so secret a matter.

"It's hard to tell you. You know I want to marry you—afterwards. I couldn't do any of this without you."

"What are you talking about—I mean, what's 'this'? After what?"

"You do want to marry me, Drusilla?"

"I—well, I don't say that I wouldn't—but—"

"Oh, do say yes, please, do."

"Suppose I say yes—but tell me what you mean by 'this.' "

"First—you know your father is to take an augury

—on the morning of Caesar's speech before the Senate tomorrow."

"Well, that's customary."

"He must find the augury evil."

I was jolted. "Predict evil? He *must?*"

"For that day. So Caesar must postpone the special meeting of the Senate."

"*Why?*"

Fuscus said—not as if he felt it but as if it were something he'd learned by heart—

"Servianus has just told me—Caesar plans to announce his choice of a successor. He knows he has not long to live—"

"Oh—no—" I moaned.

"He plans a great betrayal of his own flesh and blood! He has chosen old Titus Antoninus—instead of *me,* his own sister's grandchild! Also two *others*—and still not *me!* Not *me!*"

I couldn't open my mouth to speak.

"Drusilla! Help us now—you will be—be—empress!"

It was all too much for me. I felt myself floating away on a cloud of total nothingness.

I came to in Fuscus' arms, on the stone bench, in the heavy scent of rosebushes.

He kissed me. I was perspiring and cold at the same time.

"Drusilla," he complained, "you mustn't faint now; you're confusing me. Try to clear your mind. It's simple. All you need do . . . tell your father you've dreamed of black snakes. . . . Then, go to the augury. Just as your father begins to utter the augury—after he makes the regular observations of the way the birds are flying, and the entrails on the altar—then you cry out, you scream—black crows will be flying overhead. Everyone will see the evil omen; your father will be frightened for you—he will declare an evil augury—and the Senate meeting will be postponed until the next day. Then—I shall become Caesar—it is my right—and *you*—"

Fuscus kissed my hand; his lips felt heavily wet and repulsive; I thought of black snakes indeed—and I feared I might really dream of them.

"Promise," he begged. "Promise. I'm doing it for —for you, Drusilla." But I couldn't believe him.

"My head's bursting," I pleaded. And that was no lie. "I've got to rest—and think—"

"It is the gods' will! Else why was I born?"

"Go away now. I—will—send you—a message."

"No. No messages. There's no time for messages. Only speak to your father—remember to cry out—"

Fuscus pressed my hand. "Drusilla—for *my* sake—"

I stumbled back into my room, and Fuscus went I don't know how or where.

Aunt Chloe was at my door. "Well—well?" she whispered. *"Has he proposed?"*

I was so thankful she knew no more than that!

XVII

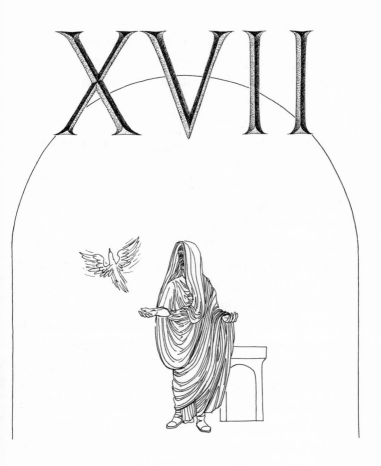

In the morning, with head still dazed, I was careful
to be early at the ceremony of the augury.

Of course I had not said a word to my father. It
would have worried him terribly, and besides, the
very request of Fuscus, and his coming to me pri-
vately, would have been a bad omen, and would

have made father predict some evil to come. Father takes those things quite seriously, though so many of the young people of Rome today think augury is a very dubious matter.

I myself have doubts, but after all, the gods have no direct way to speak to us, as they did in the past, and so perhaps they do signify the future through making the birds fly to the left hand for evil, or to the right for good fortune, and all the other incidents or counterincidents.

Father seemed in quite a good mood as he stood there in front of the altar, very imposing in his long white robe with the hood pulled over his face in awe, at the invocation of the gods.

The crowds were cheerful, too, in the spirit of all the celebrations, and awaiting the sea-fights in the Colosseum, which was even now being flooded. It was a beautiful day, the sun coming out graciously as if the gods on Mount Olympos wanted a clear view of Rome in this year of rejoicing.

Father had released the doves and was watching the sky, the hood turned back from his face. All seemed to be going well; the doves had flown to the right, and he was just about to deliver the augury, when the strange thing happened!

Out of a clear sky, one, then three, black crows were suddenly seen to be flying swiftly toward the doves. They were flying from the left, and now they crossed the path of the doves, which fluttered terrified away.

A man in the crowd shouted,

"Alas! alas! the black crows—they came *left*ward! flying from the roof of the Capitol!"

Then a woman cried,

"Yes—they were sitting on the new Mausoleum —they came from among the cypresses planted around the tomb of the Caesars!"

A loud moan began among the crowd.

My father looked startled, almost stricken, he turned pale, and frowned deeply; I could see he was reconsidering what to say.

Of course, if he so decided, an experienced augur like my father could always explain away any sign he did not feel truly significant; he could announce countersigns; he could have persons arrested for calling out or doing anything else to interfere with the auguries.

But quite probably he himself had been upset, and aware of something going wrong.

It was obvious that a troublemaker had been at work, and not an insignificant one either. I could almost see father deciding that this would not be a good day for the Senate to meet or for Caesar to announce his future successors, if only because the people would now be in an ill mood.

And he made the decree of postponement.

The Senate meeting was put off to the next day.

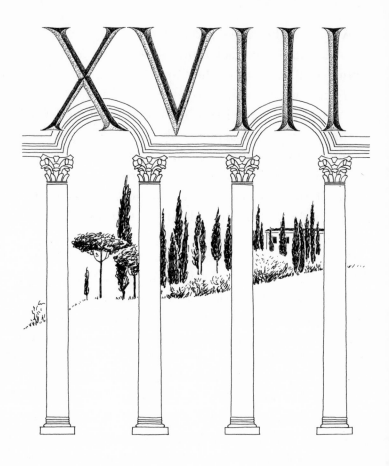

I ran home, not waiting for anyone to take me.
Whom could I dare to tell?
Whom *must* I tell?
Father?
Marius?
Yes—it must be Marius.

And there he was—hurrying out of our garden gates. He caught me as I stumbled in.

"Drusilla—you're ill!"

"No—terrible headache—I'm in a turmoil—"

He frowned, paled.

"Your Aunt Bibi's out looking for you at the augury. Your Aunt Chloe said you're ill."

"Marius—let's go in. No, I'm not ill."

How simple and decent Marius—everyone at home—looked to me after that awful talk with Fuscus.

What *were* those people up to?

What difference could it possibly make if Caesar went to the Senate and made his announcement today or tomorrow?

Surely—Hadrian was not dying?

Or—*was* he?

I told Marius. The whole story. It didn't seem fair to me, at first, to tell on poor Fuscus—then all of a sudden I didn't care at all what Fuscus felt.

Marius' face changed to absolute unbelief.

He looked at me as if I were telling him a dream I had had.

Then he knew that I wasn't.

His face fairly twisted with puzzlement.

"Why? Why? I can't figure it out. Fuscus isn't clever enough—of course Servianus is behind it—and others. But why? Why do they want this extra day so desperately? Why were they willing to prom-

95

ise you anything—of course they'd never let him marry *you* if he were to become the heir. What *for* do they need this day? To clinch supporters? It's not enough, one day. To bribe the army?—Evil predicted—a quiet day of inaction—everything relaxed before a great event—"

Suddenly Marius gave a cry.

"Great gods! I see it! I see it!"

"See what?"

"Of course!—It's murder!"

"Marius—what are you—murder—*who?*"

"Him! Him! Who else?"

"Antoninus? Annius?" I couldn't grasp it.

Marius grabbed my wrist, rushed me to the balcony and down the steps.

"Run, run—you little fool—don't hang back! We've got to run—it could be too late already!—Servianus—made the same—kind of plot—twenty years ago—"

He raced me down the stairway, through the flower garden and the back garden, talking as we flew along by the nearest way through the street toward the Palatine Hill and Caesar's palace.

"Plot—against whom?" I still wanted to know.

"Him—*Caesar! before* he can make the announcement to the Senate of his choice of heirs—and then —in the chaos—seize the government—no heir named—Servianus can claim—Hadrian—named Fuscus—"

96

As we clambered breathlessly up the hill toward the residential side of the palace and the garden where Caesar usually took his ease, I was wondering why practical Marius was dragging *me* along, when I could only hamper his running. Then I saw why.

Guards ran forward to stop him—but when they saw me, and recognized the head augur's daughter, they looked surprised but let us pass.

We ran into the imperial garden.

And do you know what?

We were too late.

Too late by about ten minutes.

XIX

Marius checked me quickly and heavily, with his hand on my wrist, as we came struggling through the thick rosebushes that bordered the path.

On a marble bench, not twenty paces off, sat the Emperor. He was breathing hard. One hand was clasped around the hilt of a sword. He was sitting on that sword. He did not notice us. His cheek was twitching.

Before him stood a disheveled man in a soldier's dusty and patched red tunic. The man was panting, gaping, gasping, flailing his arms. His hair stood up in wild black and gray masses on his greasy-looking head, his hairy face was caked with old dirt.

Suddenly a group of Praetorian guards rushed down the path toward Hadrian; they seized the old soldier with furious cries and curses, beating him, twisting his arms as he struggled wildly.

"Let him go," said Caesar, sharply.

Astounded, they hesitated, slowly released their grasp. The man stood, glaring at them and rubbing his arms, already bruised.

Caesar spoke again.

"The man's not sane. He attacked me. I took away his sword. He's harmless now."

"Caesar—he may attack again—"

Hadrian shook his head.

"I know the man. Old soldier. Pierced in the brain by an assagai, border-fighting in Mauritania years ago. He got that blow rushing between me and a huge barbarian. Didn't you, Caius? Saved my life, didn't you?"

The man began to laugh, waggled his arms, babbled and rubbed the back of his head.

"So what the devil made you come at me now, you old fool?" Hadrian demanded. "You thought

I forgot to reward you? Are your brains really gone so bad you didn't know your old general better than that?"

Caius began to cry; huge tears poured down his dirt-creased cheeks. Caesar went on,

"I hunted for you, after the battle. You were reported dead. Why didn't *you* come to *me?*—Well, it's all right now. Just tell me now who found you."

Caius stood still, trying to think.

"You were probably telling everybody what a rotten fellow Caesar is. You'd like to kill him. Eh? Weren't you? Well, *I* would too, if I'd been treated like that!"

Caius nodded his head violently.

Caesar pulled the sword from under his thigh, offered it to Caius!

"Want your sword back?—You're an honorable fellow, Caius. Caesar knows. Caesar's going to give you everything you want.—Gallus."

One of the praetorians stood to attention.

"A gold solidus."

The guard looked embarrassed. "Caesar—I—"

"Spent your pay already," said Hadrian. "Yes, I know. Your grandmother died for the third time, and you had to give her a worthy burial." The men laughed nervously. Another of the guards self-righteously produced a gold coin and handed it to Hadrian.

"All right. One good mark for Atrius. . . . Here,

Caius. There are going to be more of these. Lots more. All you want."

Caius came forward, snatched the coin and put it into his cheek, giggling with delight. Caesar was examining the sword.

"Good steel. Engraved hilt. Didn't steal it, did you, Caius?"

"No! I'm a Roman soldier!"

Caesar grinned. "No recommendation." The guards laughed again. Then, as if carelessly,

"Who gave it to you?"

"Servianus . . . Senator. Gave me. Gave me, himself. Mine."

The soldiers stared, gasped. Gallus suppressed a strong exclamation, catching Caesar's fierce eye.

"Got to give it back to Servianus now, haven't you?"

"No. No. *My* sword."

"But he gave it to you to kill me, didn't he?"

Caius nodded.

"Didn't he?"

"Yes."

Caesar handed Caius the sword.

"Caesar," Gallus exclaimed. "The evidence—"

"The evidence of an insane man doesn't count," Hadrian said, calmly. "I don't need it."

He stood up, put his arm around the wretched Caius.

"Come along, old fellow," he said. "We both need

a good lunch after all this violent exercise. How about a good old tetrapharmacum pie—like the old army days, hey?" But I saw tears shine in Caesar's eyes!

"Hooo!" Caius gloated, smacking his lips.

And they walked off, together! But the Praetorians were clustered around them, Gallus' gaze fixed on that sword.

Marius and I, watching still from the rosebushes —we thought no one had even noticed us—looked at each other, and we almost smiled. How could people be so right—and so wrong—as both of us that day?

I must admit that Caesar used some words that I really cannot repeat; let us call them soldier-language, no doubt common enough in the army, but I don't think a lady could put them down without a blush.

I'm rather surprised at Caesar: he is always particular about behaving so that people respect him as a person. But after all, he has been in military life a lot.

In spite of my father's approval of my going to Caesar, all the rest of yesterday Marius spent arguing with me. He is afraid for me, he is sure it will only make Caesar angry; he might even suspect me. *Me!* I laughed. I shot back impatiently,

"No—I don't care for *any* political arguments—

I don't care what anyone says. Aren't there any human beings any more, only politics, politics?"

"That *is* human beings—"

"No! All I see is, Fuscus has no one, no one, on *his* side. He never did have anyone. And now they want to kill him—*kill* him—all because there's no one to feel what he's been through. I'm positive the Emperor wouldn't do it if he only knew."

"Drusilla—they'll laugh at you. Caesar—*he* might even—"

"Let them laugh at me. Let even Caesar—but he won't. I can't bear to think of it—and how can even *you,* Marius? Fuscus turned from a living, hopeful person into a dead thing—and by no fault of his own—and this crime done by one of the best human beings on earth! It mustn't *be.* I'm going to Caesar!"

Marius set his lips, shook his head, gave a big helpless shrug of his shoulders, and turned away.

Yet, now, actually sitting here waiting, actually knowing that in a short while, in a few minutes now, I shall be alone in the presence of the Emperor, Caesar, Commander in Chief of all the Legions, master of the Roman Empire—and that the very life of Fuscus will be hanging upon my ability to present his story, and to convince Caesar—the great lawyer, the great statesman, the great administrator of the Roman world . . .

To convince *him* that *I* am right . . .

Oh, why did I ever start this . . .

104

But what I am going to tell him is *truth*, pure, simple truth—and he can surely never be sorry if he finds out the truth in time to save from punishment a citizen of Rome, a man so young, a man of his own flesh and blood.

It wouldn't be like our great Hadrian to resent that!

And I must. I must, for Fuscus' sake.

I must because I'd never respect myself again if I let fear for myself turn me away from trying.

And I must because—it's too late to turn back.

My attendants have touched me on the arm.

One has said, "Lady, it is close to the ninth hour."

The other, "Lady, we have brought up the litter to carry you to the Palatine. Here it stands, ready."

Oh—if only I had asked Marius to come with me—! or father! Oh, if only I weren't going to be alone!

"Lady Drusilla Vera Aureliana, daughter of the senator and head of the Sacred College of Augurs, Lucius Drusus Verus Aurelianus."

Caesar's personal attendant Diotimos was announcing me. But this time, before the doors of the imperial chamber opened, a woman I'd never seen before came forward; she was middle-aged and obviously of the servant class; her eyes were sharp as the points of a stylus, and they raked me over as if I were a wax tablet she was writing on; she went all around me, and then without a "permit me" she even dived her scratchy fingers into my bosom! But since Diotimos was permitting it, though he did not look at me, I said nothing. She bowed then and went out.

I was already frightened half to death; my heart was banging like a strong hawk father once caught and put into my hands for a moment.

Coming forward into the chamber, I made a deep salutation, my knees shaking so I could hardly rise, and when I looked up I found I was looking directly at Caesar himself. No one else was there; the room appeared shadowy, with many pillars, and two great marble busts, Plotina and Antinous, one at each side, seemed to gaze at each other across the space.

He was standing there in the simple uniform of an ordinary Roman foot-soldier, the red cloth tunic with metal plaques, and the leather sandals; he was always easiest in that dress. I'd never realized he was so tall and so powerfully muscled.

He looked heavy and tired; the wrinkles now seemed to have set deeply in his forehead; his face was pallid.

My foot touched the edge of a huge long lion-skin that lay across the marble floor, with monstrous head and bristling mane and big frightening green eyes staring out.

I started, and moved impulsively toward Caesar. He smiled involuntarily, took my hand by the fingers and drew me over to the broad couch. He motioned me to sit down, but I could only sit on the very tip of it; he continued slowly pacing the floor.

After a while he said,

"Well, Drusilla, and who is the young man?"

I stammered in surprise. He smiled.

"When a young lady is so anxious to speak personally to me, it is usually something to do with a young man. Either his marvelous virtues have been strangely overlooked, or he is in trouble. Who is it? What's he done? And what is it that I ought to do to save him from his just deserts?"

He stopped directly in front of me. I remembered that Diotimos had warned me to cut it very short; Caesar is not as patient as he used to be.

"My lord Caesar—" I got to my feet—"It is not a simple matter. May I—speak?"

"It is what you are here for."

"Oh, Caesar—it is about—Fuscus."

"*Fuscus?*"

The one word—and I felt the walls shattering around me. I felt myself a gnat on a giant's fingertip. Then, "Explain."

Without daring to look at his face, I fastened my

thoughts on the memory of a young boy, half-angry, half-laughing, bruised on the arm—a boy crying, alone, in a rainy garden—a boy hoping I would tell him he was not too ugly—a boy afraid of everyone and mostly afraid of himself—a boy without any high ambitions, begging his hateful guardian to spare the life of a rival—and now doomed to die.

I told Caesar all this.

"Sit down," he said, grimly.

But I was crying, and I fell at his feet instead.

He moved away.

"You are a child," he said, from a distance. "A child can be very dangerous, by the very fact of its limitations." He came nearer. "That innocent boy, as you call him, is the grandson of my own sister. You forgot to remind me of that." There was something in his tone that made me shiver. "If you were not the daughter of Drusus Versus . . ."

But then he laughed a little. "Well, Drusus isn't the first man to spoil an only daughter. But because you *are* the daughter of a Roman, a senator, and a man I trust, you are worth an understanding.

"Fuscus, you say, is innocent. How innocent? He knew, by your telling, that a—" his voice actually faltered—"murder was being plotted, on the ship. He did nothing to prevent it."

"He was afraid of Servianus—"

"Yes." His voice was heavy with contempt. "Fuscus was always afraid for Fuscus. You, apparently, cared much for him. Yet you must have known something of his behavior with women."

Meekly I spoke. "He—asked me—to marry—him"

"Did Fuscus ever send to speak with your *father* about marriage?"

How had I been so blind? And then I remembered—*when* he had asked me.

"Do you not understand that this weak, timid fellow—even if he were a good man, which you may yourself realize now that he is not—would become first, the tool, and then the victim, of evil men who would without regret destroy the peace of the world, the prosperity of Rome, in order to gain power for themselves? Without doubt he would succeed me as emperor, if he were to live, and perhaps soon—the lives of Antoninus and Annius Verus would not long stand in the way of such men as would become the masters of Fuscus . . ." He stopped.

"Diotimos!" he called.

"It is over," I thought, and my blood felt like ice in my veins.

"Give me that key," he ordered. Diotimos looked inquiringly at Caesar. "Yes. the key of the prison chamber of Fuscus."

Diotimos bowed low, backed out, and came back in a long minute with a large key, which he handed to Caesar.

And Caesar handed it to me. I almost kept him

waiting before I took it, a heavy, rough, iron, sickle-shaped key.

"Because I believe, Drusilla, that you, descended from one of the Founding Fathers of Rome, now understand the stakes, I give you this key. Diotimos will bring you to the prison of Fuscus. You may, if you so decide, open that door, and release upon the Roman world the future Emperor Fuscus."

I stood, dumfounded, while Caesar walked away into an inner chamber.

The key was in my hand.

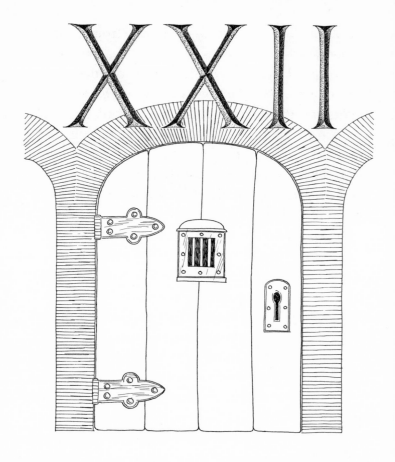

Yes, I stood with Diotimos within the huge, gloomy massive Mausoleum, at the entrance to a long corridor of heavy doors, prison doors, where persons of importance were lodged to await judgment.

And one of those rooms held Fuscus.

And I had the key to release him.

Diotimos was walking slowly in front of me; he looked back, saw that I had paused, and beckoned me to follow him.

I followed. The key was terribly heavy in my hand.

There was a silence behind the door at which he stopped.

He looked at me for a long time.

"Lady Drusilla . . . why do you hesitate?"

"Is—Servianus—in there, too?"

"No, Lady."

And still I could not lift that key to the lock.

Terrible questions were over-running my mind.

I had never thought of it before. Why *hadn't* Fuscus warned the Emperor that Servianus was plotting the death of Antinous? And, curiously enough, at this moment my mind's eye was seeing again the imperial chamber and the two great marble portrait-busts, one of the Empress Plotina, wife of Trajan, and the other of Antinous, as they seemed to gaze at each other across the chamber, and I was noting how much alike they were—and a strange thought startled me but I had no time now to think it out . . .

If Fuscus had ever thought seriously of marrying me, how was it possible that he had never sent to speak with my father? Truly, I had never actually deeply wanted to marry him . . . but had he been laughing at me? And if, *not* wanting to marry me,

113

why then had he proposed to me, there outside my room, the night of the great festival banquet, when he tried to make me promise that my father would prophesy evil and postpone the Senate meeting?

Had it not all been part of the plot to murder Hadrian and make Servianus emperor? Had not Fuscus been trying to use *me* as a tool for Servianus? Yes, even though he hated and feared Servianus? Me!—my love his tool for murdering our glorious Emperor!

My blood leapt in sudden fury.

Was *this* the man I had been wanting to save? The man to succeed great Hadrian as ruler of Rome?

I threw the key at the feet of Diotimos.

"Take it away! take it away!" I cried. And then I vomited like a puppy all over my dress and the floor.

The grim young face of Diotimos broke up into a happy smile.

"He didn't think you would use it," he said. "Caesar understands everybody."

He picked up the key and wiped it off.

"Oh, heaven," I said, sickly, leaning against a pillar and wanting to die. I stayed there, resting, a while. "Yet—I wish he had not made me—the one to be the killer—of Fuscus. That's what—I've done —now."

"You *are* easy," said Diotimos. "*Girls!*" he muttered.

He was putting the key in the door.

"No! No!" I exclaimed.

But now he was pushing the door open.

There wasn't a thing in the room.

I stared, dumfounded, at Diotimos.

"They were both executed last night," he said, matter-of-factly. "Their bodies are lying on one of the imperial sarcophagi, down below. You may see them if you want to."

"No. Oh, no," I shuddered.

A glimmer of brass at the side revealed to me now several of the Praetorian Guard in the hallway.

From behind them came Marius.

I fell into his arms, crying like mad. He embraced me hard, wiping my face with a part of my stola.

"Ugh, you are a mess, Drusilla," he said, trying to sound severe. "Wait till I wipe off that sloppy little mouth."

"I . . . I threw up. I'm sorry—"

"I'm glad. It shows you're truly over it." He wiped my lips clean, and then he really kissed me, till I heard the guards snigger, as they walked away.

POSTSCRIPT

There is nothing in DRUSILLA that could not have happened. The basic facts did happen; the rest could have. Actually, Drusilla and her family are the only fictional characters. Some permissible liberties have been taken with date and place.

As for the character of Hadrian, so much disputed, his biographer, B. W. Henderson, describes him as "foremost among the master builders of Rome's golden age . . . his wisdom ensured the happiness and security of his time." Modern historians agree.

About Drusilla, we must realize that a Roman lady of that historical period would have been taught to forget personal feelings and humanitarian motives when the good of the state seemed to be endangered.

Sulamith Ish-Kishor

ABOUT THE AUTHOR

Sulamith Ish-Kishor was born in London, where several of her poems were published by the time she was ten. After settling with her family in New York City, she studied history and languages at Hunter College. Always a prolific writer, Miss Ish-Kishor has contributed articles and fiction to many magazines, including the *New Yorker, Saturday Review, Reader's Digest,* and *The New York Times Magazine.* Her books include the popular CHILDREN'S HISTORY OF ISRAEL, AMERICAN PROMISE, A BOY OF OLD PRAGUE, (chosen as the outstanding children's book of 1963 by the Jewish National Book Council of America), THE CARPET OF SOLOMON, and OUR EDDIE (1970 runner-up for the Newbery Award).

Temple Israel
Minneapolis, Minnesota

IN MEMORY OF
ALICE SCHWARTZ NEMER
FROM
DR. GEORGE & TOBETTE DOROSHOW